YOU'VE GOT
TO HAVE
THE HEART

YOU'VE GOT
TO HAVE
THE HEART

SUE WELFORD

You've Got to Have the Heart
LL00693C
ISBN 1 85503 158 2
© Sue Welford
© cover Ted Lazlo Design
All rights reserved
First published 1992
Reprinted 1993, 1995, 1997, 2001

LDA, Duke Street, Wisbech, Cambs, PE13 2AE, UK

1

A Job at the Gym

Ben 'Tarzan' Baron must have heard me talking to Sue Baker. I had been telling her about my weekend job at the new Riverside Sports Centre. I don't know how he knew otherwise, unless one of his mates heard me. There always seemed to be one or other of them hanging around in the cloakroom at school.

'You been dreaming again, Arnold?' Ben Baron's admirers sniggered. They were always with him. Wherever he went, they seemed to go too. There were a couple of them, right hoodlums they were. Brothers – Mick and Dave Mills. I suppose they thought being with Ben made them look tough too. In fact, they stuck to him like Siamese twins. They giggled at his remark like the stupid creeps they were. 'Not body-building coach are you?'

Baron looked me up and down. He smirked at my clothes. My scruffy school trousers with hems that flapped round my ankles like sails in the wind. My school jumper that had gone out of shape. He put his finger under my grubby tie and flicked it out from the V-neck of my jumper. It hit me on the nose. I would have given anything in the world just then to be a few inches taller and broader. Not that I would have hit him or anything. I don't believe in violence. Passive resistance is more in my line. It's just that if I *had* been bigger, he wouldn't be saying those things to me in the first place.

As it turned out, 'No' was all I managed to mumble in answer to his stupid question.

'What kind of job is it, then?' he asked with a laugh.

'Find out,' I growled.

Baron laughed. 'I know, Arnold. You really mean you've got a job at the Riverside old people's home?' Baron looked at his cronies. They all laughed.

I didn't think he was funny at all. In fact, I didn't answer him again. I just ignored his stupid remark. In spite of his muscles and blond good looks, I found Ben Baron very easy to ignore. Pretending things don't exist is a good way of forgetting your fears, I've found. Not that I was *really* afraid of Ben Baron. I just liked to pretend he wasn't around, that's all. Seeing him always reminded me of my own shortcomings. I mean, he is 5 feet 10 and I'm 5 feet 6. He's got broad shoulders, bulging biceps and a broad chest. My shoulders are a bit like a plastic coat-hanger, and my chest seems to curve in, not out. His hair is thick and golden. Mine is lank and kind of mouse-brown. He rides a brand new Panther mountain bike. I scoot around on an old racer that's had three owners, none of them very careful either. Need I go on? And it's not even as if he's all body either. He's got brains as well.

But who needs guys like Baron anyway? We can't all be perfect. It just gets up my nose that Baron's more perfect than anyone else, that's all. And as for calling me Arnold, well Puny Mooney would be a better name for me. It's a wonder Baron hasn't thought of it. I suppose if I did get the chance to stand next to Arnold Schwarzenegger then the top of my head might just about reach his elbow.

I hadn't actually told Sue I was going to be a cleaner at the Riverside Sports Centre. You know, sweeping the stairs, emptying the bins, things like that. There didn't really seem to be much point. I don't suppose for one moment she thought I was going to be an American Football coach. I thought it to her credit that she didn't ask me what my job was. Mind you, Sue is a feminist. No doubt she would have approved of a bloke doing the kind of job women are usually expected to do.

The trouble was that Baron had started working out in the gym at Riverside as soon as it opened. I knew it would only be a matter of time before he spotted me. What would I do then? I decided it was a risk I had to take. If he got a kick out of calling me names, then there was nothing I could do about it. What did names matter anyway? I suppose I should be pleased he called me Arnold. Arnold wouldn't be at all pleased to be called Darren Mooney, though – would he? But if I was to go on that school trip to Spain next year I needed to earn some dosh. It wasn't any good asking my mum for it. She hardly earned enough money for us to live on as it was. It wasn't her fault. Her job at the supermarket didn't pay enough to keep a dog happy, let alone provide money for trips abroad.

I had heard Ben Baron talking about himself (as usual) one day when I was in the school loo. He was boasting to one of his sidekicks. I kept pretty quiet so he wouldn't know I was in there.

'Of course,' I'd heard him say, 'serious body-builders like me are too good for the school gym.

4

You need proper equipment to build yourself up to competition level.'

I resisted the temptation to make noises like I was being sick. I could just imagine old Baron flexing his muscles in front of the only bit of the boy's cloakroom mirror that hadn't been kicked in by some maniac. Creep!

Sure enough, I had only been working at Riverside for a couple of days when who should turn up? You've guessed it, Tarzan himself. His dad had dropped him off at the back door. Of course, it had to be the moment I was emptying a rubbish bin.

'Hey, Arnold!'

I could tell he was pleased to see me. The grin on his face was a mile wide. I knew too that I looked pretty stupid in my baggy blue overalls and red baseball cap, but he didn't need to grin quite like that.

'I like the gear,' Ben said. He fingered the badge on my breast pocket, the one with 'Cleaner' written on it. 'Did you have to pass a test to get that?'

I almost said his green and purple shell-suit

looked like a girl's. I decided not to waste my breath. I thought his pure white trainers were right over the top too, but I didn't say that either. Not that I think Baron would have done anything about it. If there was any thumping to be done it was usually left to the dreaded Mills brothers. And, just for a change, they weren't around. They were probably off pinching someone's car or breaking into the cigarette machines. Dave had already been suspended once for smoking at school and Mick was always in trouble of some kind or other. I'm surprised they both haven't been expelled by now.

In fact, all the time Ben Baron was being rude to me I didn't say a single word. Why? Because to tell the truth, I was so stunned by the blonde girl hanging on to his arm that my voice simply disappeared. She looked like a Barbie doll. She wore a body suit and tights. I had heard that there was a new girl at school. This must be her.

She looked at me as if someone had just dug me up.

'Tabitha,' Tarzan smirked, patting her scarlet-nailed hand. 'Meet Arnie Schwarzenegger.'

Tabitha gave me a kind of vomit-like smile and shook her blonde frizz. She didn't actually look as if she'd ever heard of the Queen, let alone Arnie

6

Schwarzenegger. She blinked so rapidly I was scared her eyelashes would fall off.

'Hi, Arnie,' she breathed. How she managed to chew that great wad of gum and talk at the same time was hard to figure out.

I didn't actually manage to answer. Anyway, why waste your breath? I just shook my shaggy, mid-brown straight hair and grinned. Strangely enough, although Baron seemed to have everything any bloke could wish for, I'd never been really jealous of him before. But now, seeing him with that Barbie doll on his arm, I could have cried all over my baggy blue overalls.

'Come on, Benjamin,' the Barbie doll squeaked. 'I'm dying to see you with those dumb-bells.' I thought if anyone should know about dumb-bells, Barbie, it's you.

Baron grinned down at her. He waved his arm. 'See you, Arnie,' he smirked.

I watched angrily as they walked up the steps into the gym. Barbie Doll's pink body suit was cut so high at the sides it looked as if it was cutting her in half. As I leaned on my rubbish bin, I had to admit she was really something. I wondered where she had come from. Maybe he got her out of one of those toy catalogues. You know, the ones that come inside the *TV Times* at Christmas. I found out

7

later she had moved in next door to him. Some people have all the luck. All we'd got next door was a bunch of kids on one side and a couple of hippies the other.

When I stepped back and tripped over the rubbish bin I was more annoyed than ever. I gave it a good kick just so it knew how I felt.

'Fancy her do you, Darren?'

It was Neville, the owner of the gym. Now, when you're talking about big blokes, here is one you wouldn't argue with for £1,000. I think he felt sorry for me. I mean, who wouldn't? No one in their right mind *really* wants a job sweeping up fag-ends, beer cans and sweet wrappers... do they? Certainly not while other blokes get to heave weights around and walk about with Barbie dolls on their arm.

I went a bit red when he spoke to me – especially as he'd just caught me kicking hell out of the rubbish bin in my anger.

I picked it up and shrugged. 'Not likely to notice me, is she?'

Neville looked at me shrewdly. 'You should do something with yourself, Darren,' he said. 'Get your act together.'

'Fat chance,' I said. I was feeling sorry for myself as usual.

'You don't have to take any stick from creeps like Ben Baron, you know,' Neville remarked.

I shrugged again. 'He doesn't bother me,' I lied.

Of course I didn't mean it. Ben Baron bothered me a lot. But I couldn't let Neville see that, could I?

I got the feeling, though, that Neville knew just what I was thinking. I guess he'd been around kids long enough to know what made them tick.

'Well,' he said, shrugging *his* massive shoulders. 'You can work out any time you like, you know.'

'What, and have them all taking the mickey?' I said. 'You should just see what I'm hiding under these overalls, Neville, old son. Nothing... nothing at all.'

Neville grinned. 'I've got a few customers who come really early,' he told me. 'Like before they go to work. Why not come then if you're shy?'

'I'm not shy,' I said. 'I just don't believe in making a fool of myself.'

Nev grinned again. He heaved his sports bag on to his shoulder. 'Well,' he said, 'I'm darned if I would let Ben Baron get the better of *me*.'

'Yes, but you're not Puny Mooney, are you?'

'And neither need you be. Remember Darren, the offer's there. I can't say more than that.'

'Well, thanks, Neville,' I said gratefully. 'But I'm saving my wages for a school trip.'

9

'OK,' he said. 'Run a few errands for me at weekends and you can work out free of charge.'

'Thanks,' I said. 'I'll think about it.'

It actually took me about half a micro-second to make up my mind. But I didn't want to look too eager, did I?

2

Working Out

I think Neville was surprised when I turned up the very next morning before school. In fact, I surprised myself. I'd thought that getting up at the crack of dawn was reserved for farmers and idiots.

Mind you, I quite enjoyed biking along by the river with no one about but the ducks and swans. The air smelt fresh and clean. For the first time for months I found myself really looking forward to something. I hummed the tune that was top of the charts. You wait, Ben Baron, I was thinking to myself. I'll show you who's got muscles and who hasn't.

The only thing that spoiled my ride was spotting the Mills brothers hanging around the school gates. There were a couple of other boys with them. I recognised one of them. His name was Jason Black. He went to Greenlands School on the other side of town. They were all messing around. I saw Jason get hold of Mick and throw him to the ground. He just lay on the pavement pretending to be hurt. Then his brother, Dave, went to haul him to his feet. I knew a bit about Jason Black. Not only was he a real slob but he was as bad as the Mills. In fact his brother was in prison for something or other. I whizzed past them at 90. They didn't even notice me. What they were all doing there at <u>THAT</u> time of the morning, I hated to think.

'I'm not usually at the gym this early myself,' Neville explained when I got there. 'But I'm expecting some low-calorie soft drinks. You can stack them in the cold cabinet for me if you like.'

'Sure,' I nodded. It sounded good to me. In fact anything sounded better than sweeping up litter and emptying rubbish bins.

I noticed Neville avoided looking at my old nylon football shorts and grubby vest. His eyes sort of slid away, if you know what I mean. I'd had them since I was about 12. Even then they'd been second-hand.

Neville showed me round the gym – told me what to do.

'Teenagers mustn't start with heavy weights, he said. 'You have to build up your stamina and strength before you begin to build muscle.'

'You joking, Nev?' I answered lightly. 'It's as much as I can do to lift a mop and bucket.'

'Trouble with you, kid,' Nev grinned. 'You ain't got no confidence.'

So, I thought, eyeing the machines, what else is new?

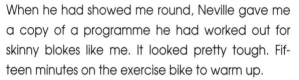

When he had showed me round, Neville gave me a copy of a programme he had worked out for skinny blokes like me. It looked pretty tough. Fifteen minutes on the exercise bike to warm up.

Warm me up, I thought? Kill me, more like!

Then you had to do four sets of eight repetitions on each machine to start. Then four sets of fifteen sit-ups to strengthen stomach muscles.

It seemed bad enough getting used to all the names. Half-squats for leg muscles. Pec-deck for chest and shoulders. Arm-curls for triceps. I felt tired just reading it.

'Now remember – only light weights to begin with,' Neville warned. 'You can build up as things get easier.'

I gulped. 'Or else I die of exhaustion,' I said.

Nev slapped me on the back. When I'd got my balance back he grinned. 'I've seen a lot of people skinnier than you,' he said. 'Don't give up before you give it a go.'

'No chance,' I said, trying to look keen.

'And don't believe all that rubbish about if it doesn't hurt then it's not doing you any good,' Nev said. 'No one does themselves any favours by straining muscles. Rome wasn't built in a day – neither was Arnie Schwarzenegger'. He grinned again.

'Right,' I said lamely.

'Don't forget,' Nev went on. 'If you're going to build yourself up, your heart's got to be in it, Darren. Same as any sport. You've got to have the heart.'

'Right,' I said again. To tell the truth, I didn't really know what else to say.

'Mind you,' he went on. 'You will be a bit sore until you get used to it.'

Oh boy – was Neville kidding! A couple of days later I crawled into the gym like some creepy alien from *Star Trek*.

'Best thing you can do is work out again,' Nev said, slapping me on the back.

When I'd picked myself up off the floor I

managed a grin.

'Did you ever fancy a job in a torture chamber?' I groaned.

Nev laughed. 'You know, I used to be a lot like you.'

I looked at him. Surely he was joking? Nev was at least 6 feet 4 and was built like a quarter-back. His T-shirt strained across the muscles of his chest and his biceps bulged over the edges of the sleeves. His collar size must have been at least 20.

'You're only saying that to make me feel better,' I moaned.

He shook his head. 'No. I started training when I was your age. I was being bullied at school and my sports teacher told me to build myself up.'

'And...'

Nev shrugged. 'And so I did. And I can tell you, the bullies soon changed their tune.'

I wondered what happened. 'Did you thump them?' I asked.

Nev shook his head and grinned. 'No. You can't deal with bullies that way. I just showed them I wasn't scared any more, looked them in the eye... know what I mean?'

I nodded.

'They could call me all the names under the sun,' Nev went on, 'and I couldn't care less. Bullies hate that. If you hit 'em, it's what they want. It's the kind of language they understand.'

I nodded again. I thought of Tarzan Baron. I knew the colour of every shirt he wore because I never looked higher than his collar.

'I don't think Baron's ever hit anyone,' I said. 'He gets other people to do it for him.'

'That's just as bad, isn't it?'

'Worse.' I said. 'It means he's a coward too.'

'That's right,' Nev agreed. 'So, kid. If I can do it, so can you. Right?'

'Right,' I said, climbing on to the exercise bike.

Neville told me diet was important too.

'It's no use trying to maintain a healthy body and eating junk food at the same time,' he said, standing beside me as I pedalled like someone in the Milk Race.

'My mum can't afford to buy steak,' I panted.

But Neville shook his head. 'You don't need steaks. Here...' he handed me a diet sheet. Fresh vegetables, fruit, skimmed milk, low-fat cheese, chicken, tuna fish, pasta – it all sounded pretty boring to me.

'But burger and chips gets boring after a while, doesn't it?' Neville said.

I shrugged. 'I suppose so.'

'Well, it's up to you, Darren. No one can make

you do it. Remember, your heart's got to be in it.'

I grinned and wiped the sweat from my forehead. 'I'll see what I can do,' I gasped, lying over the handlebars.

❖

When I gave the list to Mum, she smiled.

'I've been trying to get you to eat this stuff for years,' she said.

'So? It proves I listen to you.'

Mum was really keen about my new interest. Mind you, I think she would have been keen on anything that got me off the settee for more than five minutes at a time. She even went to the Oxfam shop and got me a track suit. It was about ten sizes too big and a style that went out when Abba were top of the charts. At least it wasn't pink and green but I almost wished it was.

The strange thing was I REALLY got to like working out in the gym. Listening to the music, getting the old adrenaline flowing. It felt good. Right. As if I had found something I'd always been looking for. And, after the first few weeks, I knew that for the first time in my life I was doing something I was really good at.

I suppose it was a couple of months before I began to see a difference. Instead of being *really* puny, I'd become just puny. Well, I couldn't expect miracles, could I?

I stood in front of the mirror every night. I don't know what I really expected to see. Neville had been right when he said Rome wasn't built in a day. Anyway, there I stood each evening before I went to bed. I bunched my hand into a fist and bent my arm upwards. Gradually, I realised there was just the beginning of a bulge in my upper arm. And when I took the muscle between my forefinger and thumb – you know what? It felt really hard. Small – but hard. Well, you can't have everything, can you? Not unless you're Tarzan Baron, anyway. After that I turned sideways and posed like you see those really big guys do in contests. I looked so funny I laughed out loud.

By Christmas, though, I could really see a change. I was wearing shirts two sizes larger and had grown out of my old football shorts and vest. And when I turned sideways and looked into the mirror I didn't laugh quite so loudly any more. I mean, I still grinned to myself. I certainly wasn't any Tarzan Baron but I wasn't Puny Mooney any more either.

Neville reckoned I was brilliant.

'You're a natural, Darren,' he said. 'If you stick at it you've got the makings of a champ.'

Yet, another weird thing was Baron's bullying didn't worry me so much any more. I mean, he still bothered me. Just the fact that I saw him every day bothered me. But not as much as it used to. Of course, he hadn't stopped taking the mickey out of me, every chance he got. In fact, I think he'd got worse. Maybe the Barbie doll was having a strange effect on him. Even his cronies didn't hang around him so much any more. Maybe they'd gone off him. I thought it would be very easy to go off someone like Baron. I suppose as he didn't have so many blokes to boss around now, he took it out on me.

'What's happened to your pet animals, Baron?' I asked him one day in the loos at school.

He looked puzzled. 'What?'

Now I'm not saying Baron had noticed I was looking different these days. OK, I got my hair cut regularly now and most of my zits had disappeared. I reckoned it must have been all the vitamins in my boring but healthy diet. But I had no trouble hiding my growing body under my scruffy sweatshirts and jeans. But what he must have noticed was that I looked him in the eye nowadays. He didn't say anything but I could tell he didn't like it.

'You know,' I said. 'The Mills boys. Haven't seen them hanging around you lately.'

Baron shrugged, 'They're off doing other things,' he mumbled.

'What ?' I said. 'Robbing banks?'

Tarzan's lip curled in a sneer. 'Anyway, Arnie, what's it to you?'

'Just curious,' I commented. I had to admit, though, I thought it pretty strange. I remembered then that I had seen them hanging around with Jason Black. Maybe they'd ditched one slob for another. Or perhaps Tarzan's Barbie doll didn't like him hanging out with thugs. Maybe she thought it was bad for his image. Things hadn't changed a bit with her, though. She was still giving me her vomit-like smiles to all Tarzan's snide remarks. She still looked through me as if I wasn't really there at all.

And as for Mick and Dave, *their* image certainly hadn't changed. They were still up to the same old tricks. I felt sorry for them in a way. Nothing to do but hang around the streets looking for trouble.

'So what are you doing with yourself these days, Arnie?' Baron sneered at me. 'Still sweeping up?'

'Get lost, Tarzan,' I said casually. He looked so stunned by the fact I'd answered him back he forgot to admire himself in the mirror.

He put his face close to mine. 'I've noticed you're getting lippy lately, Mooney,' he said when he'd recovered from the shock. 'Your important job at the Sports Centre gone to your head?'

He took a fist full of my grotty sweatshirt and pulled me close. I saw then, for the first time, that I had grown UP as well as OUT. In fact, I was almost as tall as old Tarzan. I think that shocked him a bit too. I suppose a lot of it could be that I always went round a bit hunched up before. So no one would notice I was there, I suppose. I didn't do that any more.

'So what if it has?' I remarked, not batting an eyelid. 'What are you going to do about it?'

Now, I *sounded* pretty brave but, to tell the truth, my heart was beating in my chest like one of Paul Simon's drummers.

Tarzan let me go. He looked a bit annoyed I didn't lose my balance. 'Just watch it anyway, Mooney,' he growled, wiping his hand on his jeans.

'I'm really scared,' I said, hurrying out before he could tell I was telling the truth.

The Barbie doll was waiting outside.

'Tell Benjamin to hurry up, Arnold,' she said, raising her perfectly painted eyebrows.

I opened the door again and yelled inside, 'Hey, Tarzan, Barbie Doll's waiting.'

Then I ran for it. Pretty quick. I might be getting braver but I wasn't THAT stupid.

3

Darren's Plan

One person who did notice I'd changed was Sue
Baker. Being a feminist, she came right out with it.

'You're different, Darren,' she said. 'What's
happened?'

I shrugged. 'Nothing really,' I said, thinking she
wouldn't really want to hear what I'd been up to.

'It must be that job at Riverside,' she said,
grinning. 'It's improved your self-esteem.'

'Must be,' I grinned back. 'Sweeping up rubbish
is really good for your ego.'

Sue looked cross. 'And what's wrong with doing
things like that? Some women spend their whole
lives cleaning up after people. It's a very important
and worthwhile job!'

I raised my hands to calm her down.

'I know,' I said. 'I know. Who said anything was
wrong with it?'

'Ben Baron doesn't think much of it.'

'Who cares what HE thinks?' I replied, grinning.

'You used to.'

'Did I?'

'Yes, you know you did. You used to scuttle away like a spider whenever he appeared.'

'Well, Sue,' I said. 'Maybe you're right. Maybe I have changed.'

She smiled. 'There you are,' she said. 'Never argue with a woman.'

For a feminist, I decided, Sue was all right.

❖

All this happened about the time our class had been trying to decide what to do for a Christmas show. We did one every year to raise money for something or other. Last year it was a pantomime. You can guess who ended up playing the Prince? That's right, Ben Baron. And the person who swept the stage after each show? You've guessed that too. Puny Mooney himself. I remember it quite tired me out. If we did a panto this year I really hoped I might get to be a scene-shifter or something. It would give me a chance to use those muscles I was developing.

❖

I was working out at Neville's gym three or four times a week now. I had been training since the spring and, even though I say it myself, I was really starting to look good. Mind you, I still had no trouble hiding it under my baggy sweatshirts and jeans.

In return for using the machines, I helped Neville look after the place. Cleaning the equipment, making sure the cold cabinet was kept stacked with drinks, keeping the music tapes in order, sweeping up first thing in the morning when I arrived. I began to think that if there was an exam in sweeping up I'd get top marks.

I even had my own key now. Daft, I suppose, but I was really proud that Neville trusted me.

I made some new friends too, people who didn't seem to care about my scruffy sports gear or the fact that I worked at Riverside as a cleaner. Different from the crowd of posers who used the gym at the same time as Tarzan.

In his spare time Neville was showing me a few karate moves.

'Not that I ever want you to use them against anyone,' he said. 'But knowing them will give you confidence. And if people know you know them, that's even better.'

Our Form teacher Mr Stevens (known to us as Stevie B) broke my thoughts telling us about his new idea for fund raising that year.

'What about a car boot sale?' he suggested.

'What, in the middle of winter, sir?' Pete 'Simmo' Sims shouted. 'We'll freeze to death.'

'OK,' Stevie B said, grinning. 'How about a swim across the English Channel?'

When we'd all stopped laughing he held up his hand. 'OK then, you lot. Who's got some bright ideas, then?'

Sue put up her arm. 'How about a football tournament?' she said. 'Girls against boys.'

Her suggestions met with shouts of objection from everyone. Even the Barbie doll managed to squeak in protest and wave her nail file in the air. I grinned to myself. I could just imagine her in football boots and shin-pads, up to her eyelashes in mud.

Other ideas came from all corners of the classroom.

Simmo Simms suggested a sponsored silence. That met with more laughter.

One of the girls suggested a fancy dress day.

'Mooney wears that all the time,' Baron yelled, smirking at me.

I stuck my tongue out and he made a rude sign back at me with his fingers.

Podger Smith suggested a burger eating competition. He would.

Then Mark Hamilton opened his big mouth.

'How about a beauty contest?' he suggested. He ducked down to avoid the screwed-up crisp packets and pens Sue and her friends chucked at him. Above the boys' cries of 'Yeah man' and 'Wow' and 'All right' I could hear Sue's voice. She was yelling stuff like 'Cattle market' and 'Using women as sex objects.'

The class was in uproar.

I'm surprised the Headmistress didn't appear with her red specs and in a temper to match.

Eventually Stevie B made himself heard.

'OK, OK, you lot,' he shouted. 'How about having a Miss Ashvale School and a Mr Ashvale School contest. How does that grab you?'

Sue and her friends' yells of objection were drowned this time. Laughs and shouts of agreement came from the rest of the girls as they turned in their seats to hurl rude comments at the boys.

Across the other side of the classroom I saw Ben Baron smile. Besides Sue's crowd, the only two really objecting were the Mills. But then they were the type of people who objected to everything.

I saw Dave look at Mick and curl up his lip. If it had been a sponsored shoplift they'd have thought it was brilliant.

I'll say something for our teacher, Stevie B. He really threw himself into our fund-raising project that year.

Posters appeared all over town. Mum said there was even one up in the supermarket window. I thought it must look really weird amongst the adverts for Brooke Bond tea and fish fingers.

Stevie got tickets printed and gave us each some to sell. I sold some at the gym. Mum took the rest to work and sold them all.

Stevie booked the DJ and got the lighting together. He even had a whip-round in the staffroom and bought two silver cups to give as prizes to the winners. One would look great on Mum's sideboard, I thought stupidly when he brought them to school to show us.

'If it's a success we might make it an annual event,' he announced in Assembly.

Ben Baron's eyes lit up. I bet he was imagining his name on the boys' silver cup already.

'If any of you want to come and drool over

these cups,' Stevie B said, holding them up, 'they'll be in the glass display cabinet in the front entrance.'

At lunchtime I went to look. Who should be there but Tarzan, standing with his nose almost pressed against the glass as if he wanted to get in there with them.

'You going in for it, Arnie?' he asked. He grinned as if he thought the idea was crazy.

I was going to keep him guessing.

I shrugged. 'I might.'

He laughed loudly. 'It's not a cup for the school wimp,' he said. He clenched his fist and flexed his biceps in my face. 'It's a cup for men.'

'Yeah?' I said, my face on a level with his. 'What's your name on the list for, then?'

Although it wasn't usually his style, I think Baron might just have tried to hit me if Stevie B and the caretaker hadn't come out of the Head's office just then.

The caretaker looked really angry and went clumping off down the corridor.

'Aren't you two in my maths class?' Stevie asked, frowning.

'Yes, sir. Just got to go to the loo,' Baron said. He picked up his bag and hurried off. He was still laughing. I thought maybe one day I might *really* make him laugh on the other side of his face.

Mind you, I did think about what Neville always said about it being good to put my aggression into something positive. After an hour's weight-lifting and exercise I felt really great. That's the thing about weight training. You have to concentrate so much it clears your mind of everything else. All your worries, your fears... they all seem to disappear. The only important thing is the weights... your body... the music thumping out with the rhythm of your heart. Then, of course, there's the challenge to do better each time. That keeps you going more than anything.

At times like that, thinking about Tarzan hardly bothered me at all. It was just sometimes, in the cold light of school, I really couldn't help it. He got right up my nose.

4

The Mills Brothers

As I walked along the corridor with Stevie, I noticed he looked a bit worried.

'What's wrong, sir?' I asked.

'Another theft,' he said.

'Oh? What now?'

I knew stuff was being pinched from school all the time. Two video recorders had gone missing the week before. A month ago someone had broken in and nicked three computers from the lab. And kids were always having their purses and wallets stolen. The thieves were never found. I had to admit I'd got my own ideas. I kept them to myself, of course. You can't go round accusing people of things with no evidence to prove it.

'The caretaker's keys,' Stevie growled. 'Stupid man left the door of his cupboard open. If they're not found, all the locks in the school will have to be changed.'

'Crikey,' I said.

To tell the truth, it was all I could think of to say.

People who wanted to enter the Miss and Mr Ashvale contest had to put their names on a list on the notice-board. Someone had added Ms Ashvale and written Sue's name underneath. She didn't think it was a bit funny.

'I'm blowed if I'm having anything to do with it,' she fumed, scrubbing it out. 'I'll just give some money to famine relief and have done with it.'

I rattled on again about it all being pretty harmless fun but she wouldn't listen.

Of course, people put daft things on the list. Names like Madonna and Tina Turner. Someone even put Marilyn Monroe. Then there were Nora Batty and Dame Edna – I was quite looking forward to seeing THEM in swimsuits.

I suppose the blokes had to compete by putting stupid names too. Superman, Captain America, Rocky Balboa, King Kong, Sly Stallone. Someone even put Stevie B, but that was soon rubbed out. Some idiot put Tarzan and we didn't need three guesses to know who THAT was.

And when I sneaked in one break time and put Arnold S, some people in our class *pretended* they thought it was me!

The next evening there was a football match at the Riverside Sports Centre. I had been asked to work overtime. To be honest, I was shattered, what with working out in the mornings, getting my schoolwork done AND having to bike four miles to and from school every day.

I'd told Neville.

'Rubbish,' he'd said. 'Look at you, Darren. You're a different bloke from what you were six months ago. Don't give up now.'

I'd assured him I wasn't going to give up.

'I just feel I could sleep for a week,' I'd moaned.

Nev had smiled and given me one of his slaps on the back. These days, I didn't even lose my balance.

'If you're going to win your contest, you've got to keep at it.'

I'd grinned. 'Win. You've got to be joking, haven't you?'

On the way home from the Sports Centre after the football match I noticed Mick and Dave Mills hanging around outside the kebab house. They were with a crowd of other kids, Slobbo Jason Black amongst them. It was the haunt for people that hung around the streets at night. The pavement was always a real mess – discarded bits of lettuce and onions, it made your stomach churn.

'Hey, Mooney,' they called when they saw me cycling past.

I stopped. 'What?'

Dave came across the road. 'What you up to this time of night?' he asked. He rested his fingers on the handlebars of my bike.

'Some people have to work,' I said lightly, remembering what Neville told me about looking people in the eye.

'Still sweeping up?'

'You've guessed it,' I said.

'Mug's game that,' he sneered.

I shrugged.

He let go of my handlebars. 'You're in luck tonight, Darren,' he said. 'Got other things to do than hang around talking to wimps like you.'

'Ditto,' I said.

He glared at me and I wondered what he was going to do. Then his eyes slid away and he went back to have a word with his brother. They both turned to look at me. I felt fear creep up my spine.

Just as I was about to pedal rapidly away, a bashed up old Ford Fiesta pulled up just in front of me. I was quite glad it blocked my path. My legs were shaking so much, I thought I might lose my balance and collide with the pavement if I rode off straightaway. That would have made me look a right twit in front of everybody. I sat there a minute, taking deep breaths.

Someone called out of the window of the Fiesta and Jason Black went over to talk to him. So did Mick. Then he called Dave.

Then a strange thing happened. Jason got hold of Mick and Dave's arms and bundled them into the back seat of the car. Then he got in the passenger side. The Fiesta drove off like a bat out of hell. It went off so fast half its back number plate fell off with a clank.

The crowd of kids hooted with laughter and began kicking it around the pavement.

I rode away thinking it was quite good to see someone pushing the Mills boys around for a change.

Even though it was late, I'd promised my mum I'd pick up some magazines for her from my aunty in Mabledon Road. Amongst them was one about health and beauty.

'Didn't know my mum read this kind of stuff,'

I said, grinning at my aunt.

'Neither did I,' she said. 'But she asked me to save it for her.'

I shrugged. Who was I to argue? If my mum wanted to read about health and beauty, then she wanted to read it. I stuffed the magazines into my school bag.

I'd just passed the school on my way home when the dreaded Mills brothers and their friends shot past me in the white Fiesta. They must have been doing 90. I felt sure the coppers were chasing them.

But nothing else came past so I thought no more of it.

5

Stolen Money

It was a few days before the big night that the disaster happened. Everything was ready. The Mayor had agreed to be guest of honour. The catwalk had been set up... the lights... the loudspeakers. Some of the fifth-formers had got together and formed a dance troupe. They were going to perform before the contest started. Just to get the audience warmed up, I suppose. Some bloke from the local Garden Centre had donated a huge Christmas tree to stand at the end of the catwalk. Several of us had stayed late to decorate it. It looked great: the glass balls and red and silver tinsel sparkled under the spotlights. Miss Emery who takes needlework had covered an old box with a gold cloth, ready to go under the tree. Stevie B was going to bring the cups from the display case and stand them on it.

All the tickets for the contest had been sold. Dave Mills had got rid of his to his mates from Greenlands School. I was surprised they even *knew* about the contest. We thought they were probably intending to boo everyone off the stage or start a riot or something. Whatever happened, though, we were sure nothing in the universe was going to ruin things.

Stevie B had invited six old folks from the Riverside Home to act as judges and... surprise, surprise ...they had agreed. To Sue's disgust, half of them were women.

'It really is only a bit of fun,' I'd assured her when we'd stopped off at McDonalds on the way home from school.

She had glared at me from under her glossy, chestnut fringe. 'It's not my idea of fun.' She sucked her milkshake, her brows creased in a frown.

'You can't say it's sexist – not with boys and girls taking part.' I eyed my Mc-chicken burger and fresh salad with distaste. Sometimes I really longed for a nice, juicy Big Mac and loads of french fries. I swallowed a mouthful of milk and tried not to think about it.

Sue nodded grudgingly. 'I suppose not.'

'Well, then...?' I grinned at her.

'I'm still not coming,' she insisted.

'It's up to you...'

She looked at me shrewdly. 'Are you going in for it, Darren?'

'What?' I said lightly. 'Miss Ashvale?'

Sue punched my arm and giggled. 'No, stupid. The muscle-man bit.'

I laughed. 'What do you think?'

She eyed me again. 'I dunno. You've... sort of grown lately, Darren.'

'Yeah,' I said. 'Grown more stupid.'

I was dying to tell her. But it was no good. If I didn't keep my plans to myself it would spoil the whole thing.

Just then a crowd of kids from Greenlands came in, pushing each other around and generally making a row. They sat behind me and Sue.

'Come on, Darren,' Sue said, picking up her school bag. 'Let's split.'

As we walked past them I saw Slobbo Black sitting with them. I wondered if he was haunting me. Everywhere I went he seemed to go too. He was trying to get his mouth round two Big Mac's at once.

He put out his arm and stopped Sue walking by.

'Hi, Sue,' he said, his mouth full of food.

'Oh...' Sue said, acting as if she hadn't noticed him before. 'Hi, Jason.'

'What you doing in here?' Jason swallowed. He looked me up and down, obviously deciding I'd crawled out of the woodwork.

'What's it look like?' Sue said, shaking off his arm.

He grabbed her again. 'Who's this wimp?' he said, looking at me again. I wanted to tell him he had a bit of lettuce stuck to his chin but didn't have the courage.

'Darren Mooney,' Sue mumbled.

'I know...' Jason's broad face lit up. 'Arnie Schwarzenegger, isn't it? Saw you the other night on that high-class bike of yours.'

'No,' I said, trying to stop my stomach from screwing up into a ball. 'Actually, it's not.'

Jason looked at his mates and grinned. Then he stood up. He still held on to Sue's arm.

'If I say it's Arnie, then it's Arnie,' he sneered.

'And I said it's not.'

I took a deep breath and looked him in the eye. He had a big zit on his forehead. It looked like one of those marbles with a black speck in the middle. I could see his nostrils flaring as he breathed angrily. He frowned, holding my stare. Then, suddenly, he grinned and sat down again, turning sideways to make a face at his friends.

'If you don't let Sue go,' I said casually, 'she's going to miss her bus.'

Jason turned back to say something else to his friends. Then abruptly he let her arm drop.

We heard them all laughing as we walked through the door.

Outside, Sue punched my arm.

'Ow!' I said in surprise, rubbing the muscle.

When I looked at her, her eyes were blazing.

'I don't need YOU to fight my battles, thank you, Darren!' she shouted.

Then, without another word, she left me standing there.

I spread my arms wide but she had gone. I scratched my head and sighed. Women!

I saw Sue run to catch the bus. All I could do was stand there and watch it pull away.

Sighing again, I hitched my bag on my shoulder, unlocked the chain on my bike and started for home.

When we got to school the next morning we were called to an assembly. I'd been for my usual

41

work-out and hardly had time to shower and change before I heard the bell go.

The Headmistress stood on the stage looking at us through her red-framed specs.

Sue nudged me.

'What's going on, Darren?' She frowned as she looked at me.

I shrugged. 'How do I know?'

She nudged me again. 'Why's your hair wet?'

'I've just been in the shower.'

'Haven't you got one at home?'

I couldn't think of an answer quick enough so I just nodded. Sue frowned again. I decided I'd better be careful. If *anyone*, even Sue, found out what I was up to then I knew it would get back to Tarzan quick as lightning. It wasn't that I didn't trust her or anything. It's just better to be safe than sorry.

I became aware the Head was going on about something.

I nudged Sue this time.

'What's she on about?' I whispered.

'The money from the tickets,' Sue hissed. 'It's been pinched!'

6

A Surprise Gift!

There was uproar in the hall when the Head told us that. Some of the girls started crying. I felt most sorry for Stevie B. He was slumped in his chair on the stage all creased up like a big sheet of brown paper. I suppose his job was hard enough as it was, trying to teach the likes of us wallies. Without THIS happening.

Everyone went around that day looking as if their best friend had died. Well, they would, wouldn't they? All that hard work. Flogging tickets, practices, getting things set up. It all seemed for nothing.

The police came and talked to us all. Looked for fingerprints, stuff like that. They said whoever had done the robbery must have known what they were up to. There was no sign of forced entry. The police decided the thieves must have had a key.

Now that was really strange, because the care-taker's keys had already been found.

'Maybe they had copies cut,' Simmo Sims piped up. Simmo fancied himself as a bit of an Inspector Morse. We usually took the mickey out of him but this time he was probably right.

'Why do that, though?' I said. 'Why not just keep the real ones.'

Simmo had shrugged. His claim to being a hot-shot detective didn't stretch that far.

'So they wouldn't get the locks changed, stupid!' Podger Smith said in between mouthfuls of his Mars bar.

I think we all treated him with a new respect after that.

'I'd like to get hold of whoever did it,' Tarzan said, puffing out his chest. He thumped his fist into his other hand. 'I'd teach them to go pinching our money.'

You're not the only one, I thought.

I noticed the Mills brothers didn't join in. They just hung around by the rubbish bins, looking shady.

On the way home from school I called in at the gym. Nev was there, pumping iron.

I sat behind his desk, knocking back a can of Diet Pepsi, waiting for him to finish.

Finally, he came over. He wiped the sweat from his brow with a towel. He undid his huge leather weight-training belt and slung it on the chair. He grinned.

'What you doing here this time of day, Darren?' he asked. 'Doing an extra work-out ready for the big night?'

I told him about the money being stolen.

'That's really bad news,' he said, looking glum. 'Have they told the police?'

'Yes, but they say there's no hope of getting it back. They've been looking for fingerprints and stuff.'

Nev shook his head. 'Will you still hold the contest?'

'Have to – people have bought their tickets, they'll expect to see something for their money. It's not their fault it's been pinched.'

'Tell you what,' Nev said. 'I'll have a whip-round in the gym. Try to raise something towards the charity. What do you think?'

I slapped HIM on the back. 'Thanks, Nev. That's great. I...'

'What?' Nev asked, looking at me shrewdly.

'I'd really like to know who pinched that

money, that's all.'

'What would you do?'

I shrugged. 'I don't know really – tell the police, I suppose.'

I knew that however much I had changed, hitting people would never really be my style.

When Mum came home from work that evening, I told her what had happened.

'How on earth did anyone manage to break into the staffroom?' she asked. The staffroom was where Stevie B kept all the money that had been raised for famine relief.

I shrugged. 'No one knows. The caretaker's keys were pinched last week but they turned up a day or two later.'

'What do you mean, turned up?'

I shrugged again. 'Someone found them in the car park in the shopping mall.'

Mum frowned. 'How strange. How did they know they belonged to the school caretaker?'

'They had his name and address on the key ring.'

'Oh,' Mum shook her head. 'Well, I don't know, Darren. It really comes to something when you youngsters can't raise money for charity without someone stealing it.'

'I know,' I said helplessly.

It was really stupid, but I felt like crying. All that hard work – for nothing.

Even Sue had been upset when she heard the news. I asked her if she was going to cry but she looked at me with such scorn I wished I hadn't opened my big mouth.

From what people said, I knew I wasn't the only one who'd got a good idea who pinched that money. But you couldn't go around accusing people without any proof, could you? And proof I did not have.

'What's going to happen now?' Mum asked, patting my shoulder.

'We're going on with the contest.' I made a face. 'What else can we do?'

'Maybe someone will own up,' Mum said.

I laughed. 'Don't be daft, Mum. Who on earth's going to do a thing like that?'

She lives in a bit of a dream world, my mum.

Then I thought *I* must be dreaming because she opened the sideboard drawer and took out a package.

'Here.' Smiling, she thrust it towards me.

'What's this?' I took it and turned it over. Then

47

I squeezed it to try to guess what was inside. Whatever it was, it was pretty small. 'Been to the Oxfam shop again?' I said lightly.

Then I felt sorry for saying that. I knew Mum hated not being able to afford to buy new clothes. I saw a tear sparkling in her eye and gave her a quick hug. 'Only kidding, Mum,' I assured her. 'What is it? It's not my birthday, is it?'

Mum grinned. 'Oh Darren, not even you would forget your own birthday, surely?'

'You never know,' I said.

'Well... go on then,' she said, her eyes shining. 'Open it!'

You'll never guess in a million years what it was.

A tiny pair of red satin pants.

'They're posing pants,' Mum explained. 'I sent away for them out of your aunty's magazine. All the body-builders wear them.'

I gulped in horror. I knew exactly what they were.

'I know Mum...' I said, '...but surely...'

'What?' She was looking at me with a smile.

'Mum, I can't wear *THESE*.'

I held them up. They were really tiny. Just a scrap of crimson satin held together with stitching. I held them up against the front of my jeans and paraded round the room.

When I looked at Mum she was trying to stop herself grinning.

'Mum. I can't... honest...'

'Of course you can,' she said. 'If you've got it – show it!'

'But Mum...?'

She put her arm round me. 'Come on, Darren. You've worked so hard, you can't go on stage in those tatty old football shorts now, can you?'

I looked at her and realised that for the first time in her life, my mum was proud of something I'd done.

'OK, Mum,' I grinned. 'Whatever you say!'

7

The Big Night

In spite of all that had happened, we were really excited the day of the contest. None of us could do any work. Not even Sue.

Luckily it was so near the end of term the teachers were in a good mood. We spent the morning mucking around, then most of our class went to the hall to set out the chairs ready for the evening.

A few people's dads were there doing the lighting. The DJ had set up his gear at the back of the hall. It looked really brilliant. A purple cloth was draped around the catwalk and, under the Christmas tree, the box with the gold cloth on was waiting for the cups to be brought out from the display cabinet.

At least *they* haven't been pinched, I thought gratefully.

We were allowed home early so that those

involved in the contest could get ready.

'You coming tonight then, Arnie?' Tarzan Baron asked as we were going through the school gates.

'Yep,' I said lightly.

His eyebrows went up. 'Yeah?'

'Stevie B's given me a job to do,' I said.

He grinned. 'Oh yeah? We need someone to sweep up afterwards,' he said, turning to grin at Barbie, who was clinging to his arm as if someone had spilt the superglue.

'Yeah,' I said. 'Well, I'm really good at that.'

'Oh, do come, Arnie,' Barbie Doll breathed. 'You wouldn't want to miss me in my swimsuit would you?'

You know something? She was right!

❖

I had arranged with Neville to go to the gym about 6.30 to pump some iron before the contest. I knew Baron and a few of the other guys were going to use the school gym for a change. I bet they thought they'd catch cold or something cycling to school in this weather after sweating in the gym. It was a risk I'd got to take. At least I was in no danger of them seeing me. That's the last thing I needed – my cover blown right at the last minute.

I think it was the best work-out I'd ever done. Twenty minutes on the bike and not even out of breath. Arm-curls. Leg-press. Pec-deck. Half-squats. Full squats. Shoulder-press. Lunges. Neville put my favourite music on the tape deck and for a whole hour I was in another world.

When I'd finished, Nev came up to me. He'd got his best suit on and was picking my mum up to take her to the contest.

He looked me up and down.

'Well, Darren, old son,' he said holding out his hand. 'There's no doubt about it, you've really got the heart.'

I wiped the sweat from my face and clasped his hand. 'Thanks, Nev,' I said. 'For everything... you know...'

I felt a bit awkward saying that. I just wanted Nev to know how grateful I was. If it hadn't been for him I'd still be Puny Mooney having trouble lifting a mop and bucket. 'I'll try not to let you down.'

Nev shook his head. 'Even if you come last you won't have let anyone down.'

I stood at the top of the steps and watched him climb into his XR3. His massive frame hardly fitted in the driver's seat. If I'd had a brother I would have liked it to be him.

It was ever so cold that evening. There was a threat of snow in the wind. I pulled my hood up over my head and put on my gloves. Cycling along to school, the cold air felt like breathing in knives.

When I got there the whole place was like a ghost town. Round the back of the boiler house I saw the beat-up white Fiesta that belonged to Jason Black's friend. It was easy to tell it by its broken number plate. I groaned. The last thing we really needed was *his* rough mates messing things up. It looked as though someone was sitting in the driver's seat but I was in too much of a hurry to get a good look.

I parked my bike, hitched my tatty sports bag over my shoulder and made my way to the front entrance. In the light from the lamp I could see my breath coming out like grey fog. I glanced at my watch. It was 7.45. The fifth-form dance troupe would be just about beginning their routine. They were due to be on stage for half an hour before the contest started.

As I went through the doors I heard the dull thump of rock music echoing down the corridor like far away thunder. I looked at the display cabinet and saw the cups were gone. I could just imagine them shining under the Christmas tree. I bet Tarzan could see one shining on his sideboard already, big-headed creep that he was.

It could have been my imagination but the figure of a girl just going into the hall looked like Sue. I had tried to persuade her to come but she had refused. I decided it must have been somebody else. I could just imagine her at home, watching something boring on telly and missing all the fun. It was daft but I would really have liked her to see me on that catwalk. Even if I did make an ass of myself.

I jogged along the corridor and up the stairs to the boys' cloakroom. There was no one in there either. I breathed a sigh of relief. I knew they were all going to get ready early so they could watch the girl's contest first. If I didn't hurry up, I'd miss it too.

I took the fastest shower in the history of the world and put on my red satin pants. I didn't dare look at myself in the mirror. If I did, I knew my courage might fail me altogether. I put my old baggy tracksuit back on and stuffed my sports bag into my locker. By now, it was 8 o'clock. I knew Stevie B would be doing his nut looking for me. I was supposed to be backstage, making sure everyone had turned up. Luckily, the entrant 'Arnie S' had been drawn to go on last.

I scooted back along the corridor and down the stairs, two at a time. At the bottom I stopped suddenly. I listened. Above the steady thump, thump of the music from the hall I could hear another, strange noise. Then, when there was a lull in the drumming, I heard it again. I stood there frowning. It seemed to be coming from the care-taker's cupboard under the stairs. I went round cautiously to have a look.

There was no sign of anyone but I could hear shouting. The door was shaking where someone inside must have been thumping it with their fists.

Then I heard what they were yelling.

'Help! Help! Someone – let us out!'

I waited until they stopped for a minute, then I shouted back.

'Who is it? Who's in there?'

They began to shout louder. 'Get us out, get us out!' They began banging on the door again.

'Who's us?' I knelt down and shouted into the keyhole.

A voice I THOUGHT I knew shouted back, 'Just get us out of here, will you?'

I looked round but there was still no one about. Time was getting on and I knew I'd be late if I didn't get a move on.

'OK,' I said. 'Stand back, I'll try to force the door open.'

I stepped back a bit. I took a few deep breaths then ran full-force at the door. I slammed my shoulder against it as hard as I could. No one was more surprised than me when it busted opened and I fell right inside. I flew into the three people who had been locked in. We all fell together in a heap. I heard a lot of swearing and cursing and there seemed to be a lot of arms and legs waving in the air.

When I'd got over the shock, I sat up and rubbed my shoulder. I reckoned it would be bruised for a month.

Then, when I saw who had been in the cupboard, even though it seemed I didn't even know my own strength, you could have knocked me down with a flipping feather.

8

A Shock for Darren

I think the three of them were just as shocked as I was. We all sat there just staring at each other. Tarzan looked really stupid. He had obviously been ready for the contest when someone locked him up. His gold lamé robe was creased up and his hair was all out of place. He gazed at me with his mouth open.

'How...?' he started to say.

I just went on rubbing my shoulder and looking at HIM. I could hardly believe my eyes. What on earth were Tarzan Baron and the Mills brothers doing locked up in the caretaker's cupboard, for goodness' sake?

Then Tarzan jumped up and shouted, 'Mooney – the cups have been pinched. We've got to get them back!'

'What...? Pinched...?' I was still dazed. 'Who...?'

Dave Mills scrambled to his feet. 'It was Jason Black, he made us tell him where they were, then shoved us in here so we couldn't raise the alarm.'

I stood up, and saw for the first time that I was taller than either of the Mills creeps. I looked first at Dave, then at Mick.

'What, Baron too? Jason MADE Baron...' I couldn't help it, I began to grin.

'He was in the cloakroom when Jason came in and started pushing us around,' Dave explained, giving Baron a dirty look.

I must have looked really amazed then. I mean, who wouldn't?

'Pushed you around...' I grinned. 'The great Tarzan Baron?'

Baron's eyes slid away from mine. I knew there was no time for him to explain now. I didn't really know if I wanted to hear anyway. All I knew was, our cups had been nicked and the great strongman Baron hadn't been able to do a thing about it.

'Anyway,' I said to the Mills creeps, 'what do you mean he MADE you?'

They both went red. 'He...'

'You may as well admit it,' Baron sneered. He was busy trying to brush the creases out of his robe. 'You do everything he tells you to do.'

I turned quickly. 'What... you mean like they used to do everything YOU told them to?'

'It wasn't me who got them to pinch the care-taker's keys so someone could take a copy of them and break into the school...'

So Podger Smith had been right. I looked from one to the other. To tell the truth, Baron looked a bit sheepish – as if he knew someone had found out at last what kind of person he really was. It wasn't hard to look sheepish, though, not for someone with a face like his! In fact, I'd always wondered what he reminded me of.

Suddenly aware that the whole evening would be ruined completely without the cups, I took hold of Dave by the front of his jumper.

'OK,' I said. 'When and where...'

'Just now...' Dave stammered, looking scared. 'We'd only been in here a minute...'

It only took a few seconds to tell me the rest.

❖

I knew I hadn't passed Jason Black on my way in, so I figured he must have gone round through the junior school.

I gave Tarzan and the creeps one dirty look and belted off down the corridor. I'd realised something else. That Fiesta parked round the back of the boiler house had been waiting for someone. Now I knew exactly who!

Luckily I knew the layout of the school like the back of my hand – should do, I seemed to have been going there for almost all of my life.

I whizzed past the Head's torture chamber and into the canteen. The ladies getting the grub ready for the interval looked at me in surprise.

'Evening all,' I grinned and ran through the middle of them. I didn't even turn round when several pots went clanging to the floor.

I wrenched open the back kitchen door and rushed out through the stores, down the covered way and through the boiler room. I hurled myself through the door just in time to see Slobbo Black getting into the passenger seat of the Fiesta. The engine was already revving.

I threw myself at the door and grabbed the handle.

'Hey!'

I pulled Jason Black out by the hair.

'Ow! Leggo, you...'

He tried to get back into the car but I held on like death. I could feel the hard muscles of my forearm knotted across his windpipe. He made a kind of strangled grunt. I released the pressure.

'OK,' I said grimly. 'Where are those cups, you creep?'

Then I felt someone grab me from behind. I twisted away and landed him a flying drop-kick in the stomach. Neville didn't really want me to use karate moves but I reckoned this was the time for them. The man doubled up, yelling. Then it sounded as if he was being sick.

While this was going on, Jason was trying to stuff something underneath the car seat. I grabbed him again.

To my surprise, he held up his arms to ward me off. A big slob like him, scared of old Puny Mooney? I could hardly believe it myself.

'OK,' he cried, 'OK. Take the stupid cups they're a load of rubbish anyway.'

He grabbed them and threw them at me. I caught one, but the other went spinning away underneath another car.

Really angry, I lunged for Jason again but he skipped aside and ran off across the car park. I started to belt after him but decided he wasn't worth the effort.

The other bloke was still sitting on the ground holding his stomach.

I took hold of the back of his jacket and hauled him to his feet. When I saw his face, I knew

61

straightaway who he was. He must have been released from prison. Like his brother, Jason, he had a face like a weasel.

He twisted away and I was left with his jacket in my hand. I chucked it aside and grabbed his arm. He shook his head and tried to get free.

He bent double, coughing and spluttering again. That's all I need, I thought to myself, this creep throwing up all over my tracksuit.

Looking at him made me feel ill so I shoved him to one side. A slob like him wasn't worth missing the contest for. I'd got the cups, even if one was a bit dented, that was all that counted. I suppose revenge is pretty sweet, but victory must be sweeter still. I picked up his jacket and was going to throw it at him when I realised it felt really heavy.

I looked at him, then at the jacket. Then I looked at him again. He stretched out his arm.

'Gimme...' he began.

I shook my head slowly. Then I put my hand in the inside pocket. My fingers closed over a poly-thene bag. A heavy polythene bag. I felt coins... notes... and I knew straightaway what it was. I drew it out.

'That's mine...!' he began. He lunged forwards but I held my arm up high.

'Oh no, it isn't yours, you creep,' I sneered.

I threw his jacket into his weasel face. 'This is the money we raised for famine relief. It was YOU the Mills brothers got those keys for, not your slobby brother!'

I knew I could easily have hit him hard. But, as Neville had told me, thumping a rat like him wouldn't have solved anything.

Instead, I took several deep breaths and clenched my fist until my nails dug into the palm of my hand.

'You'd better scarper,' I said quietly. 'And I shouldn't go home if I were you. When the coppers hear about you they'll be down on you like a ton of bricks.'

He gave me a filthy look and climbed into his car. He shot away so fast the rest of the number plate fell off.

I crawled under the other car to retrieve the dented cup and went back into school.

On my way to the hall I passed Tarzan. He'd combed his hair and got the creases out of his golden robe.

He didn't look even me in the eye when I gave him a grin as wide as the sky.

Backstage, I found Stevie looking pretty desperate. He was talking to the DJ.

'It's all ruined,' he was saying. 'First the money. Now the cups. Those kids have worked so hard. If only I knew who had...'

'Sir,' I hissed, 'can I have a word?'

'Darren!' He turned to look at me. 'For God's sake, where the hell have you been? You were supposed to be here hours ago!'

Then he saw what I was holding and his mouth almost dropped to his knees.

'Darren! Where the...?'

'It's a long story, sir,' I said, grinning. Then I fished around in my pocket and handed him the bag of money. 'I've got this back too.'

I think if he hadn't been our form teacher he might have wept. He just slapped me on the back and gave me a sort of shaky grin.

'I don't know if it's all there, sir,' I said, thinking Jason's creepy brother might have spent half of it. 'But it's better than nothing.'

'It certainly is, Darren,' Stevie B said softly. 'It certainly is.'

We just stood there a minute grinning at each other. Then Stevie seemed to come to his senses.

'Put the cups under the tree, please, Darren.' He waved the bag at me. 'I think I'd better hang on to this, this time.'

'Right, sir,' I grinned.

'And then start checking the entrants, will you? They're all lined up, ready.' He handed me a clipboard with the list of names typed on a bit of paper. The name 'Arnold S' seemed to stand out in letters of fire. I felt my insides begin to screw up.

'Yes, sir,' I said again. This time it was my voice that was shaking.

I crept out front and stood the cups beneath the tree. I put the dent round the back so no one would see it.

When I was backstage again, I heard Stevie go out in front of the curtains and say something to the crowd. Then there was a lot of cheering and clapping but I don't know what it was all about.

Then the music started up and the contest began...

9

On the Catwalk

They held the girls' contest first. There were all sorts, all sizes and, it goes without saying, all shapes.

I don't think the panel of judges from the old folks' home could believe their eyes.

The mood was great. Music thumping out, cheers and clapping from the audience. Even the Head was clapping like mad. I bet it was the first beauty contest she'd ever been to. She'd never entered one, that was for sure.

The DJ put on Tina Turner singing 'Simply the Best' when the Barbie doll made her entrance. I don't know if someone had bribed him or something. There was a weird kind of silence. As if the audience, the teachers, the parents, could not believe what they were seeing. I noticed a woman in the front row wearing what looked like a blonde wig, and a bright green catsuit. She was sitting with her hand over her mouth. It had got to be her mum. No one else would have a Barbie look-alike for a mother. And the man next to her looked like one of those guys out of Thunderbirds – you know hair greased back and kind of wooden expression. That had just got to be her dad.

Tarzan's Barbie teetered up and down the cat-walk on heels as high as the Eiffel Tower. I'd got to admit, though, she looked pretty stunning in that kingfisher satin bikini. The spotlight picked out glints of gold in her frizzed hair and caught the silver in her long, dangly earrings.

The amount of clapping and cheering that took Barbie off stage left everyone in no doubt as to whose vanity unit the girls' cup should be sitting on later on that evening

The judges took about two seconds to make their decision. The Mayor gave Barbie the cup and put this satin sash round her. 'Miss Ashvale School' was printed on the sash in purple letters. Barbie blinked her false eyelashes at them, then waved to the crowd. I wasn't the only one who almost burst out laughing when she tripped down the steps.

After the interval it was the guys' turn.

I was still hanging around backstage in my baggy tracksuit. I had been ticking off the names as the entrants did their bit. Stevie B had been going around calling for Arnie S but no one seemed to have turned up. Good job he was the last to go on.

A lot of the guys had only entered their names for a laugh. Hoots of laughter greeted their entrance. I could see my mum almost falling off her chair laughing when they did their poses. I guess she was thinking of me when I first started. Would you believe it, though, some of them were even skinnier than I had been.

The most amazing thing was, though, from where I was standing I could see someone else – Sue, of all people. She was lurking at the back of the hall, trying to hide behind one of the pillars. Her curiosity must have overcome her ideals after all.

It was daft, I know, but I felt really pleased she'd decided to come.

I'd made sure everyone, except old Arnie S, was lined up to take their turn, then put down the clipboard.

'You needn't hang around any more, Mooney,' Tarzan commented. 'Go out front and enjoy the show. Don't get too jealous though, will you?'

'I'll try not to,' I said lightly. 'Throw up!' I added under my breath.

Of course, when Baron went on things became

deadly serious. They played the music from *Rocky*.

He stepped on to the catwalk and paraded up and down. There were a few screams from the third-year girls. Then he turned to face the crowd and did a few poses. His oiled muscles gleamed in the spotlight.

He left the stage to cheers and whistles. I had to admit he looked good.

He smirked at me as Barbie put his gold robe around his shoulders. They went off, arms round each other, to gloat over the rest of the show.

Before I knew it, it was my turn. Stevie was still doing his nut because Arnie hadn't turned up.

I'd taken off my tracksuit by then.

'I'm here, sir,' I said in his ear.

His jaw fell so low his teeth almost dropped out.

'Darren!' he exclaimed. He looked at me as if he thought I'd just beamed down from the Starship Enterprise. 'Are YOU Arnie S?'

'Who else?' I said, grinning.

He wiped his hand across his brow. Then his face broke out in a wide grin. He gave me a slight shove.

'Well go ON then, Darren,' he said. 'They're waiting.'

The lights dazzled my eyes at first. They'd changed the record to some Guns'n'Roses job.

The DJ must have known it was my favourite.

You must have heard about hushed silences. Well, that's what there was. When my eyes got used to the lights I could just see several guys from the gym sitting with my mum and Neville at the back of the hall. Mum and Nev were both waving like mad. I think my mum was actually standing on her chair. Nev gave me a thumbs-up sign and all of a sudden I felt really great. I didn't care one bit if the crowd booed me off. I didn't care that Tarzan Baron and his blue-eyed dolly were standing at the side staring at me as if I was Dracula risen from the grave. I'd made it on to the stage in spite of my shaking legs and screwed-up stomach. Now I was there it was up to me not to make a right wally of myself.

I stepped on to the catwalk and after that second's hushed and truly gobsmacked silence, the hall suddenly erupted like Mount Vesuvius.

I didn't win, of course. I mean who could compete with Baron? He'd been training for a couple of years and I'd only just started. Mind you, Stevie B told me that if there had been a runner-up prize. I would have won that. It was really weird, though. Tarzan stood there holding up the cup as if it was the Holy Grail while everyone gathered around me. They slapped me on the back and said lots of good things to me, asked me about the money and the cups. I suppose that's what Steve must have been telling them about before the contest started. Later, Mum said everyone crowded round me because I'd won their hearts and that mattered more than winning any stupid old cup.

When everyone had gone, Baron came up to me. He held out his hand. I think he was a bit surprised when I shook it.

'You're really full of surprises tonight, Darren,' he said. I might have been dreaming but there was a kind of grudging respect in his voice.

'Yeah,' I answered, looking him in the eye. I leaned my arms on the handle of my broom. 'Wait until next year, Baron. Then you'll really get a shock.'

Baron grinned as if he didn't believe me.

Another surprise was that even Barbie Doll told me I'd looked really great. AND she managed to say it without looking as if she wanted to throw up.

Maybe it was the red satin posing pants that did it.

I'm going to the pictures with Sue next week.
Being a feminist, SHE asked me.
Of course.